C

I dedicate this book to Sigma and Delta, who graciously put off the invasion of earth until after publication.

THE EARTH IS FLAT

A Collection of Short Stories

Steve Lance

CONTENTS

Copyright

Dedication

Title Page

Proof the Earth is Flat — 1

Head North — 4

Sunlight Cola — 11

Ticket Please — 18

Barn Owl Court — 25

Thanksgiving Day Massacre — 30

Destination Earth — 34

Petal Power — 40

Monster Pears — 43

A Date with Destiny — 47

The Swamp Monsters and the Case of the Missing Robe — 53

Clown Island — 56

Herbert and the Monster Guild — 61

Check Please — 65

Shark Tales — 69

Books By This Author — 73

PROOF THE EARTH IS FLAT

by Steve Lance

For most of my life, I believed the Earth was round. I thought little about it. After all, Magellan had sailed around the Earth. Wasn't that enough?

Then one day, as I was taking my morning walk around the block, I realized I had started at one point and returned to that point without turning around. Now obviously, I did not walk around the world. So how did this happen? Simple answer, I walked in a circle.

Is that what Magellan did? That would have been much simpler. And is not the simplest solution usually the correct solution?

Did Magellan just make a big loop around the Atlantic Ocean? It seemed plausible.

But if I was going to change my opinion about the Earth being flat, I needed to apply some scientific rigor. An experiment that would prove the Earth was flat. I saw a basketball sitting on the ground. I realized that the basketball should roll away if the Earth was round. I needed to test my hypothesis.

I got a round barrel and laid it on its side. I put the basketball on the barrel, and it rolled off. A chill ran down my spine. Did I just prove that if a ball is placed on the surface of a round object, it will roll off? I repeated the experiment with a baseball, a ping-pong ball, a marble, and a billiard ball. All with the same results. I turned the barrel upright and placed the basketball on the flat lid. It did not move.

But I knew that if I was to publish my result, I needed to have the experiment repeated by someone else. And it should be a blind study. The scientific community is very big on blind studies. And if they were not only going to accept but embrace my conclusion that the Earth is indeed flat, my experiment had to adhere to the highest scientific methods.

I blindfolded my brother and had him repeat the experiment. Again, he got the exact same results. A 100% confirmation.

After the experiment, I explained to my brother what I was doing. He responded by calling me a moron. This further confirmed that I was on the right track. So often, when you go against what is generally believed, people call you names. I know this is anecdotal proof, but proof nevertheless.

I remembered that Isaac Newton claimed the Earth was round. But Einstein proved several of Newton's theories wrong. If you can be wrong about one fact, can't you be wrong about others?

Besides, who was I to go against Albert Einstein?

I just needed something that could not be questioned. Something that would prove beyond any doubt that the Earth was flat. Then one day in Home Depot, I saw it, a level. And not just any level but a deluxe level. Its whole purpose for existing was to show you what was flat. It was on sale, begging me to buy it. Fate had shown me the way.

I put the level on my table, perfectly flat. Then I put it on my counter, the refrigerator, a bookshelf, and a coffee table, all flat. Finally, I took it outside and lay on the ground so I would be at eye level with the little bubble that never lies. I held my breath and placed it on a small patch of Earth. 100% without question, flat.

This was proof positive. Home Depot is one of our most respected commercial enterprises. It would never sell a level that did not work. Besides, it had a money-back guarantee. Home Depot now had a financial stake in the outcome.

The Earth is flat, and I have proven it!

HEAD NORTH

by Steve Lance

"Adolf again with the dark colors, too much gray and black. Why not add color to your paintings?" said the art professor.

Adolf threw his brush down and looked up at the professor. His eyes teared up. He had been working on the assignment for the last fourteen hours. His stomach growled, and he was ready to fall over from exhaustion. "You told me to paint what I feel. To dig deep inside and let it flow out onto the canvas."

He would turn twenty-three soon and was no closer to being accepted as a serious artist. Always the same criticism, the paintings were technically sufficient but flat and emotionless. Adolf was thinking seriously of giving up art and going into politics.

"Now, Now Adolf, you will get it eventually. Let joy into your life. You are a young man. You should smell the flowers, soak up the sunshine, and court a beautiful young girl. Let love into your heart, and the rest will follow."

"I'm trying. Just yesterday, I invited Fraulein Bertha Hoganstuff to a dinner of sauerkraut and blutwurst. She spent the entire dinner shoving sausages into her mouth. And when I went to kiss her goodnight, her breath was like a butcher shop that had not been cleaned in days. It's hard to paint posies after a night like that."

The professor felt sorry for young Mr. Hitler. He was trying so hard to be accepted into the art community. But his gloomy outlook and fits of rage drove people away. Adolf needed a change of scenery. He needed to get away from Vienna.

"Adolf, your birthday is coming up. Twenty-third, I believe. Why not give yourself a gift? Take a cruise, do some traveling. You should visit America."

"Yes, a sea voyage. I could paint the stars at night and the sea during the day. I bet I could even meet a fraulein who does not smell of sausage."

"The Titanic is setting sail soon. You know she is unsinkable."

"I shall do it. I'll turn over a new leaf. I'll embrace life and all it offers. From now on, I'll only see the good in everyone and spread goodwill towards mankind. Thank you, professor. I'm off to book passage on the unsinkable Titanic."

For the first time in years, Adolf felt at ease. He spent the first couple of days out on deck painting the ocean. It was a relief not to have anyone looking over his shoulder, telling him to add more color.

A robust Texan lady named Dolly noticed the peculiar little man painting his heart out. Dolly was a sucker for men with passion. She also liked the skinny little frantic type. They reminded her of her pet chihuahua.

"Say, partner, you're quite a painter. That's the third seascape I've seen you paint today."

Adolf looked up and saw a woman at least twice his size looking over his shoulder at his painting. It annoyed him that she had broken his concentration, and he attempted to ignore her and continued painting.

"I think you might get bored painting the same old sea every day. Most artists I know like to do portraits, maybe even a few nudes. Now I'm not saying I'm going to pose for you nude. Goodness no. But if you sweet talk me a little, I might sit for a portrait."

Adolf could feel his blood pressure rising. He had been happy painting the sea. And now, a rather large woman was telling him what to paint. His eyes glowed red with anger. He turned around and said, "I don't have enough paint to create a picture of someone as large as you. I doubt there is that much paint on the ship. If you want to be painted, maybe you should wait until we dock and they repaint the hull."

Now Dolly doesn't mind a man with a bit of spunk, but this was downright rude. Her face grew red, and she said, "Why, you little squirt. I have bowel movements larger than you. I hope you're not set on making it to America because I will knock you all the way back to your little European trash town."

Dolly reached down and grabbed Adolf's shirt, lifting him a good three inches off the deck. She took a handful of his paint and smeared it on his face. Then threw him in a trash bin and walked away.

Adolf, stuck head-first in the trash bin, found himself strangely aroused. A porter, who had witnessed the incident, rushed over and helped Adolf out of the bin.

"What a woman," Adolf said.

"That is Dolly Bootenell. The richest lady in all of Texas. Been married five times. All five died of heart attacks. The scuttlebutt is that it happened during passionate lovemaking. Best you stay away from her unless you want to be the sixth. But what a way to go. If you get my drift," said the porter.

"I have never felt this much desire. It is consuming me. I must meet this woman. I will paint her. I will paint a nude of her. I will create the most beautiful nude of the most beautiful woman in the world. Where can I find this Dolly of Texas?"

"Ah, most likely at the buffet."

The courtship between young Mr. Hitler and Ms. Bootenell of Texas began in earnest. At first, Dolly, still mad from the fat remark, showed little interest. But Adolf was persistent. He arranged to bump into her at the breakfast buffet, then at the bunch buffet, and once more at the lunch buffet. And when they both reached for the last piece of fried chicken, and Adolf stopped and motioned for her to take it, the anger faded away. They spent hours talking, laughing, and taking long walks on the deck until they suddenly found themselves outside Dolly's stateroom.

"I guess we should say goodnight," Dolly said.

"It's been such a great day. I hate for it to end," Adolf said.

"Well, you could come in," Dolly said. As she grabbed Adolf and pulled him inside her stateroom.

The door closed behind them. And two and a half minutes later, Adolf came out smoking a cigarette, his hair disheveled. "What a woman," he said.

On April 14th, 1912, Dolly agreed to pose nude for Adolf. They would do it that night on the deck when nobody was around. But Adolf wanted something dramatic in the background, a giant iceberg. So he paid the helmsman to head north into a patch of water known to have drifting ice. At first, the helmsman resisted, but Hitler pointed out that the Titanic was unsinkable.

When an iceberg came into view, Adolf had Dolly drop her robe and positioned her in front of it.

"Move a little to the left. You're blocking the iceberg," Adolf said.

"Watch it, you little puke. I'll slap you around good," Dolly said.

"Enough with the pillow talk. You're getting me aroused, and I don't have a spare two and a half minutes. I must paint you while the iceberg is still in view."

"Ah, it seems to be getting pretty close. Should we tell the helmsman to turn?"

"Nein, remember the Titanic is unsinkable."

The ship hit the iceberg and scraped down the entire length of the hull. Ice came flying onto the deck, and water flooded the lower compartments.

"Adolf, did we cause that?"

"We better be going. Quick, let's get in one of the few lifeboats they have," Adolf said.

"It's women and children first. We must try to save as many people as possible. Help me round up the children." Dolly said.

"Ah, sure, yeah, right. Tell you what. You head in that direction and find as many children as you can. I'll go the other way and do the same."

Adolf rushed to his stateroom. He searched for something that would make him look like a child. He put on a pair of lederhosen with knee-high socks and shaved his mustache but, in his rush, left a small patch of hair under his nose.

Back on the bridge, the captain questioned the helmsman as to why he steered the ship into an icefield.

"So let me get this straight. A young man named Adolf Hitler ordered you to turn the ship north, and you obeyed him," the captain said.

"There was something about him. You just obeyed his orders, no matter how ill-advised they seemed," the helmsman said. "Besides, the ship is unsinkable."

"Unsinkable, that's just marketing. This ship is over forty thousand tons of iron. Of course, it can sink," the captain said.

"Why did they advertise it that way."

"What do you think they are going to say? 'Almost unsinkable,' 'It probably won't sink.' Have you ever seen a restaurant advertise 'The Tastiest burger in the world'? It's never the tastiest burger. Sometimes the burger is downright awful."

Meanwhile, Adolf was able to sneak onto a boat filled with children. As they were floating away from the ship, a little girl clutching a teddy bear stared at him.

"This boat is for women and children. You don't look like a little boy," the girl said.

"Of course, I am. My personal pronoun is junior. Now be quiet," Hitler said.

"I saw you give that man money to sail north. This is all your fault."

"Yeah, well, I could do a lot worse things. "

"You're going to have to do something pretty awful to top this."

SUNLIGHT COLA

by Steve Lance

Nobody can hear a scream in the vacuum of space, or so they say. So, when Delta floated by the portal window, Sigma simply cupped his hand to his ear, shrugged, unwrapped a frozen burrito, and put it in the microwave. You can't blame Sigma. It was the third time this month that Delta had forgotten to tether himself to the space cruiser before going on a spacewalk.

Gamma, amused by Delta's antics, flipped on the intercom. "Delta, are you trying to tell us something."

"Tell Sigma to suit up and come get me. I forgot my tether," said Delta.

Sigma seemed uninterested and continued watching his burrito slowly turn inside the microwave oven. "These earthlings create the most amazing gadgets. I got this burrito warmer at a place called Best Buy. I can have a piping hot burrito in two minutes. They measure time linearly. How quaint."

"Sigma, Delta needs you to rescue him," Gamma said.

"Tell him I'm having lunch."

"Come on, Sigma. If the captain sees me, I'll get put on maintenance duty. I won't be able to join you in invading Earth."

Sigma looked at the microwave, which had just given off a ping. Delta was his best friend, and he was fun to have along when you invaded planets. "I'll come to get you after I finish my burrito."

"Come now. When we get to Earth, I'll go to Chipotle and get you a burrito. I'll even throw in some chips."

"And two salsas?"

"Chipotle is very generous with their salsa. You only need one."

"Sorry, busy right now."

"Ok, two."

Sigma signed out a nova class star cruiser with a Boreas 680 dark matter engine and dual antimatter injectors. Fully outfitted with eight heavy-duty Deimos disruptors and sixty-four Kratos missiles. It also had a juice bar and karaoke machine containing a wide selection of Lionel Richie songs.

The invasion of Earth was sponsored by the Intra-Galactic Soda Company. Their main product Sunlight Cola, needed the excess CO_2 the Earth produces to give it that delightful fizzy taste.

Sigma named Delta second in command and gathered his senior staff to discuss the best way to conquer Earth. Sigma wore a leather jacket with the Intra-Galactic Soda Company logo prominently displayed on the back. There was a table full of swag, and Delta picked up several beer koozies.

"I say we just blast the hell out of them," said Alpha. He took a swig of Sunlight Cola and held his lips tight as he suppressed a burp.

"Only as a last resort. I want to keep the casualties low. We need as many people driving cars, heating buildings, and flying planes as possible. We have to keep the CO_2 level high," said Sigma. "Oh, that reminds me. We better kidnap Elon Musk. We don't want too many of those Tesla's cutting into our CO_2 output."

"I've been monitoring their social media," said Gamma. "If someone says the wrong thing, they get canceled. What if we pipe in all the sitcoms from the 70s, 80s, and 90s, and when someone laughs, we cancel them."

"Interesting idea. But I've seen some of those shows. Who's going to laugh at Three's Company?" said Sigma. "Who else? Delta, you always have a good idea."

Delta got up from his chair and walked over to the swag table. He picked up a tall tumbler inscribed with the words 'Drink Sunlight Cola'. He turned and paced back and forth in front of the senior staff.

"We could blow them to bits like Alpha wants." Delta looked Alpha in the eyes. Alpha lowered his head and looked away. "Or we can use their own insecurities against them. Launch a micro-aggression campaign. Start explaining the properties of dark energy, and every time they ask a question or look confused, we roll our eyes. Thereby destroying any self-esteem, they may have." Delta put the tumbler back on the table and picked up a teddy bear with an 'I' followed by a red heart and the words 'Sunlight Cola'; he handed it to Gamma. "But what fun would that be."

"Earthlings are some of the most entertaining creatures in the universe. Just last night, I was watching one of their comedy channels, it's called C-SPAN. Best deadpan humor I have ever seen. With a straight face, they were making all these hypocritical statements. They lie straight to the camera, never cracking the smallest smile. I was rolling on the floor."

"They call these masters of comedy politicians. They are so loved by the people that they let them do whatever they want. No matter how bizarre. And they won't let them retire either. It was like watching a grandma and grandpa convention," said Delta.

"This is all very interesting, but how does this help us?" asked Sigma.

"We use envy. You see, if one country has something, then they all want it. Take nuclear weapons. All the major countries have them. And many other countries are envious and trying to get them for themselves. The best part is they point them at each other and threaten to destroy the whole Earth. They call their strategy MAD, mutually assured destruction. I told you they have a sense of humor." Delta could see most of the staff was smiling and shaking their heads in support, although Sigma still looked skeptical. "When I get to Earth, I'm going to party with some of these wack jobs."

"Get to the point," said Sigma.

"What we do is take a small town and declare it to be a sovereign nation. Make it the capital of the world. Then we give it everything an earthling would want. The best schools, hospitals, airports, free power, water, internet access, and cell phones with four cameras. We build not one but two Chipotles, a fleet of mobile Starbucks that follows you around. Of course, the other countries will get jealous, and in exchange for some of our technology, we will get their CO_2."

"Why don't we just ask them for their excess CO_2? It's causing all kinds of problems with their environment. They may be happy to get rid of it," said Gamma.

"Won't work. I've heard the politicians talking. They have no interest in reducing their CO_2," Said Delta.

"Delta is right. They are doing everything possible to pump more into the atmosphere. So we have to assume it is highly prized," said Sigma. "What technology should we offer them?"

"Self-cleaning porta-potties, the ones on Earth, are disgusting," said Delta. "I say we make Chugwater, Wyoming, the world's capital. The Chugwaterers .... Chugwaterain .... those are hard to say; we will call them the Chuggers. They will become the envy of the world."

"It's settled. We are off to conquer Earth," said Sigma.

On the outskirts of Chugwater, Wyoming, Sigma landed the star cruiser, which he renamed the Enterprise. His research had shown that this was the most common name for earth spacecraft. He felt it would make them seem more familiar and give a friendly vibe.

Delta observed one of Earth's creatures squat, squeeze out an impressive duce, and wait while his servant picked it up and put it in a plastic bag. This shaggy creature must be the apex predator. "Take me to your leader," Delta said.

The turd carrier said, "Excuse me, he doesn't talk."

"Oh, you must be his interpreter. We would like to see the mayor," said Delta. "I see you collect turds. I bet you have quite the collection. You will have to show it to me sometime." Delta noted that dung would be a good gift for humans.

The turd carrier escorted Sigma and Delta to the mayor's office. Delta wanted to make a quick stop at the restroom, so he could procure a welcome gift for the mayor. But Sigma insisted that the diamond-encrusted 24k solid gold letter opener would suffice.

The mayor welcomed them into his office with a hardy handshake. He had a round face, a round body, and a wide smile. He gave a small laugh after everything he said, "I'm guessing you're not from around here, *hah, hah, hah*. I hope you didn't bring a probe, *hah, hah*. Not sure what you had for lunch, but it turned you a little green, *hah, hah, hah*. Did you hear what I said, a little green, *hah*."

As Sigma sat down, he noticed a coffee cup on the mayor's desk. One side had 'Galactic Soda Company', and the other said 'Moonbeam Cola'. "I guess we are not the first to visit you," said Sigma.

"Just this morning, we got an offer from a couple of interesting creatures," the mayor said. "They will build us a Taco Bell, right on Main street. Imagine Chugwater getting its own fast food restaurant. I guess we have made the big time, *hah, hah, hah*."

"We were thinking you might want a Chipotle instead," Delta said.

"Hmmm, Chipotle, that's one of those fancy burrito places. No, the citizens of Chugwater are a down-to-earth bunch. We start getting all uppity; next thing you know, we will be eating them fish eggs, *ha, ha*."

"Hear us out. We can offer you —."

"You heard the mayor. They want a Taco Bell," said Dos, a blob-like slimy creature. He was followed into the office by Tres, his second in command. Dos and Tres were from the planet Zit, a long-time rival of Sigma and Delta.

Delta pulled out his blaster. "Good, I've been wanting to pop a Zit."

Sigma motioned for Delta to put his blaster away. He didn't mind starting a war, but if you are too close when you pop a Zit, you get slimed. "Mayor, It looks like you have a choice to make."

"No need for all this animosity. We have plenty of CO_2 for everyone," the mayor said.

"We are not giving the Zits anything. Delta, back to the spaceship, and tell Alpha to warm up the blasters," said Sigma.

"If that's the way you want it. Let the Cola Wars begin," said Dos.

Join us next time when we find out:

Will Delta finally get to pop a Zit?

Will the Zits slime their way to the White House?

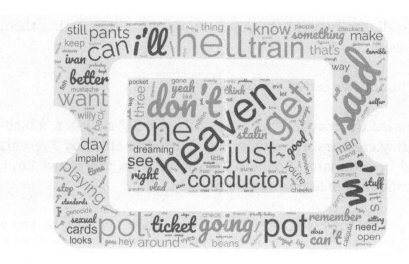

TICKET PLEASE

by Steve Lance

What a strange dream, I was flying. Time to open my eyes and start another day. Is that Stalin playing checkers with Chairman Mao? Obviously, I'm still dreaming. I better close my eyes. It doesn't feel like a dream. I'll open just one eye. Yep, Stalin and Mao Zedong playing checkers, and Stalin is cheating. It looks like we are in some type of train car. Oh no, someone who looks like Pol Pot is sitting across from me. Better close my eye. What is the last thing I remember?

I was on a bridge with my buddies, and a church bus was going by, and we were mooning them. I was laughing and remember saying, "I'm Going to hell for this." Then, as I was pulling up my pants, I stumbled and fell off the bridge. Yeah, I remember falling. It was a long way down. But how did I get on a train with Stalin? And should I tell Mao he is cheating?

"Hey you, the one pretending to be asleep. Do you want to play Go Fish?" asked Pol Pot.

Ok, this is weird. I don't think I'm dreaming, but how can Pol Pot be asking me to play cards if I'm not dreaming? "No, I'm just going to keep sleeping until everything goes back to normal."

"You're not sleeping. I dealt you some cards. Do you have any sixes?"

Hmmm, it can't hurt to peek at my cards. Let's see, oh, three sixes. That seems ominous. "Yes, three of them. Aren't you Pol Pot? The man responsible for the Cambodian Genocide?"

"Don't judge me. I'm not the one sitting here with his ass cheeks hanging out of his pants."

Oops, guess I didn't get a chance to pull them all the way up. Better make a to-do list. First, pull up my pants. Second, sit up straight and look around and see what else is strange. Third, stop using the term genocide around homicidal dictators. Forth, hand Pol Pot my three sixes. Oh good, here comes the conductor.

"Ticket, please," said the conductor.

"I don't belong here. If you could just let me off at the next stop."

"Check your pockets. I need to know your stop. Is it the sulfur pits, the lava room, or maybe the torture device emporium?"

None of those stops sound good. Let's see nothing in my pants pocket. Nope, the shirt pocket is empty. "Sorry, I don't have one. Just let me out here."

"Throw him in with all the sexual deviants. He showed up with his pants around his ankles," said Pol Pot.

"Hey, at least I didn't kill two million of my own citizens."

"Do you want me to make it two million and one?"

"This is highly irregular. What is your name?" asked the conductor.

"Willy Johnson."

"I told you he was a pervert. That's a double phallic name."

"Settle down. Just keep playing cards while I sort this out," the conductor said.

This must be the afterlife. It figures I would get stuck on a train with this a-hole, "Do you have any Jacks?"

"Why? So, you can go jack-off, pervert."

"That is it. I don't care if you are one of history's biggest mass murders. It's go time."

"All right enough. Or I'll put you in the car playing Boy Band songs 24 hours a day," said the conductor. "I figured out what happened. Despite your childish pranks. I mean, mooning nuns, what's the matter with you? You should have gone to heaven."

"That is bullshit; he gets into heaven," said Pol Pot.

"Yeah, they really lowered their standards," said the conductor. "Anyway, at the very moment you died, you said, 'I'm going to hell for this.' That's a direct quote. To make a long story short, we have a new person doing the paperwork, Jeffrey Dahmer. Maybe you know him. He got confused and put you on this train."

Cool, I get to go to heaven. The best part is I get away from Pol Pot. "I'm not happy about the mix-up. But I'm not going to make a big deal out of it. Just drop me off at heaven."

"We can't do that. Heaven won't let us in."

"Why not?"

"See that man over there? The one with the little mustache. Can you imagine what would happen if we pulled up to the Pearly Gates with him on board?"

"So, now what?"

"We are willing to let you into hell. But the problem is you need a ticket. So we need you to do something evil. That will generate a ticket, and we can just cruise this train right into hell."

"I don't want to go to hell."

"It's not that bad. I'll get you a job in the kitchen. All we ever serve is beans. You just warm up the beans every day, and it's pretty hot in hell, so actually, you just have to open them. Then you have the rest of the day to read. We have a terrific library. Have you ever read Dante's Inferno?"

"I think I'll stick with heaven."

"Heaven is not that great. They will probably assign you as a guardian angel, and you'll end up listening to people whine about their problems all day. More than one angel has ended up choking the shit out of those little whiners. They get cast out, right into a pit of sulfur. You'll be wishing then that you took the job opening beans."

"Still heaven or hell. I'm going with heaven."

"Hate to tell you, that's not an option. Either get a ticket to hell or spend eternity playing Go Fish with Pol Pot. This train can't go to heaven, and we can't slow down till everyone has a ticket," said the conductor. "Tell you what. We got plenty of time. Get to know some of the other passengers. I'll check back in a little while. Oh, one last thing, stay away from Jeffrey Epstein. I know this is a train to hell, but we still have some standards."

Not much of a choice. But I sure as hell don't want to spend eternity with Pol Pot. Ha, sure as hell, that's pretty clever; I have to remember that one. I might as well be friendly; I'll just wander around and introduce myself. There are a couple of friendly-looking gentlemen who must be from the middle ages. "Hi, Willy Johnson. I just got here."

"Yeah, we know. You're the sexual deviant keeping us on this train," said Ivan the Terrible. "I'm Ivan, and that is Vlad the Impaler. You don't want to show you're butt cheeks to him."

"Real funny, Ivan. Look, Willy, hurry up and do something evil. Lucifer is throwing a big Halloween party, and I don't want to miss it," said Vlad the Impaler.

"I'm not sure what I can do. Are you sure I can't still get into heaven?"

"Heaven, no chance. Caligula is three cars up. He always has some kind of evil, sexual deviant stuff going on. Should be right up your alley."

"Hey, it was just a prank. We were just doing it for laughs." *Caligula, hmm, that has to be some wild stuff.*

Who is waving at me? It looks like he is with Ted Bundy. He seems crazed; wait a minute. No way. I'll just be polite but keep away from him. "Hi Charles, or do you go by Charlie?"

"Yeah, go over and talk to Manson. He's good at getting people to do evil stuff," said Ivan the Terrible. "Or better yet, ask Idi Amin for some of that meat he is eating. That should get you into hell."

"Do something quick. Or I'll get one of my pointed spares out," said Vlad the Impaler.

Man, these guys are getting upset. I better do something. Here comes that man with the funny little mustache. Here goes.

"Ow, you bastard," said Adolf. "David Berkowitz just did the same thing. Why does everybody think they can kick me in the balls."

What is that bright light? It seems warm and inviting. Is that my grandma? I'll just step through and see what this is about.

"Welcome," said Saint Peter.

"Where am I now? What happened to the train?"

"You are in heaven."

"But I don't have a ticket."

"I can send you back. If you want."

"No, no, no. It's just I thought I was going to hell."

"We were just messing with you. After all, you did moon some of our finest nuns."

"Sorry about that, we were just bored and —"

"Don't sweat it. It gave us a good laugh. We have it all on YouTube. Come on, you can watch it. It's gone viral."

BARN OWL COURT

by Steve Lance

The wire-rimmed glasses, the slight graying of the feathers, his slow but deliberate walk, made it clear this barn owl was a bird of great importance. He took the judge's chair and gaveled the court into session.

"Order, order, I'll have order in this court. The first case is Micky Eugene Mouse vs. The Barn Owl Community. Is the defendant ready?" the judge said.

A disheveled barn owl raised from his seat, straightened his jacket, and said, "He is your honor."

"Micky Mouse is that your real name?" the judge asked.

A small nervous looking rodent stood up. "It is your honor, but I go by Eugene. My parents were big fans of Disney, and well, that's why they named me Micky."

"You don't share their sentiment?"

"No sir. I feel they are engaged in mouse culture appropriation. I'm hoping to change their business practices by using my middle name."

"Good luck with that." The judge rolled his eyes, and the owls in the courtroom snickered.

"Before we get started, this mouse seems a little underfed. Get him some mouse chow, fatten him up a little," the judge said.

A mummer went through the courtroom, and comments like "Good Idea", "Yeah, fatten him up", "He needs more meat on his bones", "He would hardly even make a snack" were heard.

The mouse started darting his head around. He saw the owls all looking at him. He checked the floorboard, searching for a mouse hole that he could use to escape.

His defense owl, reached over with his wing and patted him on the shoulder. He gave him a reassuring look. "Nothing to worry about. I'll make sure you get a fair trial."

"Let's get started. Prosecutor, what is this mouse charged with?" the judge said.

A young barn owl with his feathers slicked back stood up, put one wing inside his jacket, and walked back and forth in front of the jury. "The Barn Owl Community will prove that Micky Eugene Mouse stole a small block of cheese. That on or around last

Tuesday, he took a knife and cut the cheese from a larger block."

Hearing the phrase 'cut the cheese', the courtroom burst into laughter. A few owls put one wing under the wing pit of the other and started making farting sounds. This only added to the laughter. The prosecutor smiled broadly, enjoying the fact that he made everyone laugh.

"Order, Order, I'll have no more outbursts. For the rest of the trial, no one is to use the phrase cut the cheese," the judge said.

Hearing the judge say it made the court once again erupt in laughter.

"Order, defense you're up," the judge said.

"Owls of the jury, my client was gifted this cheese. The owner of the cheese told him to take the knife and cut . . . I mean, slice off a chunk for himself. There was no crime, just an act of kindness by the owner of a large block of cheese."

While the defense spoke, the prosecutor put a whoopie cushion on the defense's chair. He sat down, and a significant farting noise echoed throughout the courtroom. Once again, the owls of the court erupted in laughter.

"Order, I think we have heard enough. The jury will now go deliberate. Everyone, clear the courtroom until the jury returns. Except for Eugene, you stay there and eat some more mouse chow."

The courtroom emptied out, leaving poor Eugene alone with a bowl of mouse chow.

After deliberating for less than an hour, the jury sent word that they had reached a verdict. Everyone filed back into the courtroom only to find that Eugene was missing. Only a mouse tail was left on the defense table.

"Your honor, Eugene is missing. I found his tail. I fear the worst," the defense said.

"He must have escaped. I guess that settles this case," the judge said.

"But your honor, his tail looks like it was bitten off and spit out."

"Most likely just a fashion tread. You know, with your tattoo and body piercing, I guess cutting off body parts is the new trend. I know a guy once, cut off his whole body, just a head, turned out to be pretty inconvenient, had to roll everywhere, said it hurt."

"Your honor, I believe a crime has been committed. One of the owls in this room ate Eugene."

The owls in the courtroom started to gasp but then realized, yeah, more than likely.

"Hold on, counselor, that's a pretty serious charge. What proof do you have?"

"Well, there is his tail and drops of mouse blood. Plus, it looks like you have mouse fur in your teeth."

The judge grabbed a small mirror, saw he had a little fur, and quickly removed it.

"Let's not get bogged down in who may or may not have eaten Eugene, and remember the jury was going to find him guilty anyway. So whoever ate him did a public service," the judge said.

The jury foreman stood up and said, "Actually, we found him

innocent."

"Innocent, he is a mouse, you are owls, we never find the mice innocent," the judge said.

"We feel that has been a terrible miscarriage of justice," the foreman said.

"Great, I get a liberal jury right before lunch. Too late now, Case dismissed."

"You're honor, what about Eugene?" the defense asked.

"He was delicious. People, we are owls; we eat mice. That's what we do."

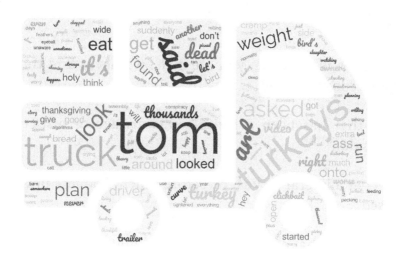

THANKSGIVING DAY MASSACRE

by Steve lance

"Holy cow, is that you Tom? What have they been feeding you?" Art asked.

"Look who's talking. Hey, I got some disturbing news," Tom said.

"Here we go again. What is it this time, hormones in the feed, cramp living quarters, not enough fresh air?"

"Worse, they are planning to slaughter us. All of us."

"Come on, Tom, really? Ever since you found that phone, it's been one conspiracy theory after another. Social media is messing with you. It's the algorithms, dude. They are just trying to get you all jacked up. It's clickbait, man, clickbait."

"Listen, I found this story on Vocal. It's all about this feast that happens once a year. At the center of it is a turkey. A dead turkey. A dead roasted turkey. They eat our flesh. They call it 'Carving the Bird'. I'll give them the bird."

"Our owners would never do that. They are good to us. They give us all we want to eat. Sometimes, I think it's a little too much. I have packed on the pounds."

"That's part of the plan. They are fattening us up."

"Hey, don't go around fat shaming. Not cool. I think I look good with this extra weight. I even heard the owners saying I was 'Looking Tasty'. Which I assume means awesome."

"Here, let me show you this video I found," Tom said.

As Art watched the video, the feathers on the back of his neck stood up. He looked over at Tom, his eyes wide open.

"Holy shit, I never saw so many heads get chopped off. What was that an assembly line?" Art asked.

"It gets worse. Look what they do after we are dead," Tom said. He showed Art another video.

"What are they shoving up that bird's ass?" Art asked.

"Breadcrumbs."

"Why would they shove bread up his ass? Who are these monsters?"

"After they roast the turkey, they scoop it out and eat it."

Art started to feel sick. His throat tightened as he did everything he could to keep from vomiting on Tom's feet.

"They eat bread pulled out of a dead bird's ass! Who are these people?" asked Art.

"Don't worry, I have a plan. In a few days, they will load us onto a large truck. We will then...."

Tom told Art the plan and asked him to tell the rest of the turkeys. So now, all they had to do was wait for the truck.

As the owner was loading the turkeys onto the truck, a few of the turkeys stared right at him, giving him the eyeball. A lot of them would not even look in his direction. A couple tried to peck him. It was all very strange. Normally the turkeys are happy to get away from the cramp barn, but these all looked pissed off.

As the truck was rolling down the highway, Art said, "You all know the plan; there is a tight curve up ahead. Everyone throws their weight to the right side when we go around it. You all look nice and plump, so let's use that extra breast meat."

The truck driver, unaware that he was hauling thousands of turkeys willing to do anything for their freedom, did not slow down for the curve. As he went around it, he felt the trailer's weight suddenly shift. The trailer tipped onto two wheels, and the weight became too much as he made the turn. The trailer tumbled over and broke wide open.

"Run, run for your lives," Tom said.

Art looked over and saw Tom headed for the truck cab. "Tom,

what are you doing? Run."

"I've got some pecking to do," said Tom.

The truck driver, dazed but unhurt, was standing beside the truck, watching as thousands of turkeys suddenly turned and started heading for him.

"Let's get him boys!" said Art.

With Tom in the lead, Art by his side, and thousands of turkeys right behind, the truck driver ran for his life.

That Thanksgiving, millions of turkeys would still end up on the dinner table. But somewhere deep in the Louisiana bayou, there are a thousand plus turkeys, thankful that Tom had read an article on Thanksgiving.

DESTINATION EARTH

by Steve Lance

"Hey Delta, orders just came down. Looks like it's back to planet Earth," said Sigma.

"Excellent," said Delta. "I get to use my new probe, see how I outfitted it with a green light. It gives off a nice eerie glow. I call it Big Daddy."

"Why do you bother with the probes? All we are supposed to do is a couple of catch-and-release abductions and buzz a few navy planes. And the captain wants us to swing by Chipotle and pick up a couple of burritos. Crap, I forgot to ask him what type of salsa he wants."

"Hot, always make it hot," said Delta, as he continued to polish his probe. "Oh yeah, you will do nicely."

"You know, if you don't use the probe," Delta continued, "They get upset. They feel cheated, didn't get the complete alien abduction treatment. Plus, what they can charge for interviews really goes down. "

"Chugwater, Wyoming, is our target location. You do the abductions. I'll buzz the planes and get the takeout," said Sigma.

"Hey Sig, when you fly by those planes, do the thing where you're completely motionless and then shoot up 10,000 feet. That always messes with them. I love hearing them talk about it. 'We have nothing that can go that fast.' Well, no, not unless you have a Class 1 Intergalactic Star Cruiser, duh."

Delta and Sigma had been working together for several years on a hit reality show called 'Messing with Earthlings.' Sigma was a legend in the industry. He had won several awards for the work he did on creating realistic Big Foot sightings. And, of course, there was his early work, where he convinced earthlings you could not travel faster than the speed of light. Like no one ever heard of using an antimatter quantum phase shifter. The best part was that he dressed up as a human with this really wild hairdo and walked around saying stuff like 'Everything is Relative.'

Delta walked up to the residence he had scouted and rang the doorbell. While waiting for the occupant to answer, he looked around and noticed what a lovely, quiet town this was. Who knows, maybe he could retire here, get to know the town folks, and have his morning coffee with some retirees at McDonald's. It would be nice.

He realized he was holding the probe, Big Daddy. Better put it away. It makes them a little squeamish if they see it ahead of time. Best to take it out only at Show Time.

A twenty-something young woman answered the door. "May I help you?" she asked.

"Yes, mam, are you Sharon Stone?" Wait a minute, not the actress, Delta thought for a second. No, that can't be. She was abducted a while ago. You don't see her in movies anymore.

"Do you need something?"

"Oh, right to business. I like that. I'm here to abduct you. I'm an alien, and that's kind of what we do."

"Hmmm, antennas, green skin, dark eyes, freakish shaped head. Alien, you say, I would never have guessed. Sorry, today's not good for me. I have a dentist appointment. I was just leaving for it."

"Freakish head, that's a little unkind. Can't we just call it uniquely shaped? Anyway, I've come a long way. I'm on a tight schedule, afraid you have no choice." Delta thought about showing her Big Daddy. Maybe that would seal the deal, but it seemed a little too forward.

"I would love to go with you, unique head and all, but these appointments are hard to get. I'm not missing it. You should have called ahead," she said.

This would not be easy. He could always get a cup of coffee and abduct her after her appointment. After all, good dental hygiene is important.

"Tell you what, I'll go over to Starbucks. You can meet me there after your appointment. Then, I'll take you to the ship, give you a tour, do a little paperwork. I'll have you back by dinner."

"Ok, but none of that weird alien crap. Simple abduction, and then right home," she said.

As she headed for the dentist, Delta was glad he had not shown her Big Daddy.

Delta was at Starbucks for a couple of hours and was getting impatient. He was thinking about how typical it was of American women to keep men waiting. He knew that was a stereotype, but political correctness had not reached his home planet in the outer quadrants.

When Sharon arrived, she smiled and waved at him. She was carrying a small bag and came over to his table.

"I got you a present," she said. She pulled a silk tie out of the bag and handed it to Delta. "Look, it's got frogs on it. They match your skin color. When I saw it, I just had to get it for you. I'm sorry about that freakish comment I made earlier. It was early, I was in a hurry, and you caught me off guard. Anyway, your noggin is adorable. I hope this makes up for it."

Delta was truly touched. In all the abductions he had done, no one had ever gotten him a present. Tears welled up in his eyes.

"Are you crying?" she asked.

"Crying, why no, it's just all the smoke in here is getting to my eyes."

"There hasn't been smoking allowed indoors for years."

"Oh right, I thought it was 1970. You know that whole space-time continuum thing. Hard to keep track of what decade we are in," Delta replied.

Just then, Sigma came in.

"I've been looking all over for you. The captain wants to get going," Sigma said.

Delta stood up, straightened his clothes, and said, "Sigma, I would like you to meet Sharon. She is our abductee. We were just having some coffee and getting to know each other. Please join us."

"It's very nice to meet you, Mr. Sigma. I can see Delta is not the only handsome alien around."

"Yeah, whatever, come on, Delta, grab her, and let's get her to the ship. Then, you can do your thing with Dig Daddy and...."

"Ah Sigma, what's the hurry? After all, we traveled 50 light years to be here. I'm sure we have time for a pleasant lunch. Let's not be rude to our guest."

"What's Big Daddy?" Sharon asked.

"Oh nothing, that's ... that's ... just what we call the ship. He meant I could show you around the ship, which we call Big Daddy, right Sigma, Big Daddy, the name we have for the ship."

"Whatever, look, abduct her, don't abduct her. I couldn't care less, but we have to get going. You have five minutes to get back to the ship." With that, Sigma left the coffee shop.

"He was certainly rude," Sharon said.

"Oh, he's a nice guy. Just the captain has been on him. There was a whole burrito incident. He got one for the captain, but the sour cream went bad. The captain spent some quality time in the head."

"I have to go, but I would like to see you again," Delta said.

"I would like that also, Big Daddy," Sharon replied.

"Oh, no, no, no, please don't call me that. Delta will do just fine."

PETAL POWER

by Steve Lance

There have been many transformative and significant uprisings throughout history. The Marigold Uprising, led by Joseph Flowers, was not one of them. Joseph, or the Marigold Man, as he would become to be known, wanted to replace the rose as the national flower with the marigold.

It is not clear if it was his love for the marigold or distrain for the rose that drove him, but driven he was.

It had all started many years ago when, as a young man, he had fallen hopelessly in love with a local beauty known as Mary Potts. He worked up the courage to ask her to the local dance. On his way over, he purchased one red rose. He asked the all-important question and handed Mary the rose, but things went horribly wrong before she could give her answer. The rose still had its thorns, and one of them cut Mary's hand. It caused a single drop of blood to fall on her white blouse. Mary, upset that her favorite blouse was ruined, started to cry. As she sobbed, she said, "Oh, why did it have to be a rose with thorns? Why couldn't you have just gotten me a marigold."

Joseph, heartbroken, vowed he would avenge his one true love. And so his quest to make the marigold the National Flower began.

Joseph thought hard about what weapons he would use to wage this uprising. Finally, he decided this called for using the most powerful weapon known to mankind. Yes, he would use microaggression.

No more would he stand idly by when someone sang the praises of the rose. Instead, he would roll his eyes. In his bartending job, if someone wore a rose print, he would serve them last. If they had the actual flower, he would purposely get their order wrong. At the county fair, when the Best Rose contest was being judged, he made disparaging remarks under his breath. He refused to recognize February 14th as anything but a typical day and purposely wore orange.

This went on for years, and sometimes Joseph felt he was making genuine progress. For example, he cited a 32% increase in the use of orange on Halloween. He attributed this to people secretly supporting his efforts.

But for every victory, there were setbacks. They played the Rose Bowl every year, despite his refusal to watch. He wrote to the Orange Bowl and pleaded with them to adopt the marigold. His letters went unanswered. And most troubling of all, the White House continued to use the Rose Garden for important events.

But Joseph labored on. He knew one day he would succeed, then he could return to his hometown and ask Mary for that dance.

But then the event that would shake him to his very core happened. You see, Mary had not stayed in their hometown; she had left to become a successful Broadway actress. And one day, Joseph saw a flyer advertising her latest play, "A Rose by Any Other Name," starring Mary Potts.

What did this mean? Had she tired of waiting for him and was taking matters into her own hands? Was she declaring that you should no longer use the term rose? Joseph was confused. He had to get to Broadway right away.

On February 14th, 2021, Joseph Flowers, the Marigold Man, dressed in orange, purchased one ticket at the Garden Theater to see Mary Potts star in the hit Broadway play "A Rose by Any Other Name." As the show went on, Joseph grew depressed. She was not speaking out against roses, and there was no mention of marigolds.

After the play ended, during the curtain call, an event so catastrophic happened, Joseph would never recover, and his life work would lie in ruins. As Mary Potts took her bows, they handed her a large bouquet of red roses. Smiling, she accepted them, leaned over, and inhaled their aroma. She kissed the person who handed them to her on the cheek and said, "I always love getting roses, especially on Valentine's Day."

MONSTER PEARS

by Steve Lance

Herbert was not like your normal everyday monster. Oh, sure, he was a loner, like most monsters. After all, it's "The Blob", not "Blobs". It's "Big Foot", not "Big Feet". His problem was he just was not scary or could say mean things. He was constantly being hugged by children. A real problem for a monster.

Besides scoring exceptionally high on the Monster Likeability Index (MLI), he had reverse Tourette syndrome. He just could not help yelling stuff like "Have a nice day" or "Enjoy the sunshine". The biggest problem was long lines. He was always saying, "After you". It could take him hours to pay for his groceries.

That morning, before heading back to tend his pear trees and pick some pears, which he sells at a roadside stand, he dropped off his 99th application to join the Monster Guild. As usual, he had drawn smiley faces on the envelope. When handing it to the receptionist, he said, "You're looking very nice this morning. Did you do something with your hair?"

'Why yes, it is a new style,' she answered.

'Well, it looks fantastic. Have a nice day.'

Herbert hated himself for being so nice. He was a monster. He should have slammed the application on the desk, growled at her, and said, 'Make sure you don't lose this, or I'll be back, and you will pay dearly.' That's what any normal monster would have done. "Have a Nice Day" give me a break.

The Monster Guild was an organization dedicated to causing terror and mayhem throughout The Human Race. As a member, you could attend workshops such as "How to Fit Under Children's Beds" or "Advance Techniques for Appearing in Car Headlights on Moonless Nights". You could also charge Union rates and be eligible for health care. Best of all, they had recently started offering dental coverage. This last benefit was controversial. Some monsters believed that crooked teeth and bad breath made them more terrifying. At the same time, others argued that good dental hygiene was more important.

(Editor's Note: Few monsters floss daily, but a Public Service Campaign is currently underway to improve the numbers.)

Having pruned his pear trees and picked a few buckets of pears, Herbert was sitting at his pear stand waving to traffic as they drove by. Sometimes he would give them the thumbs up or try to get them to honk their horns. It was a bright sunny day, and he was all smiles.

A large black car pulled up, and a rather ugly short fat man got out.

'Hello, isn't it a beautiful day? That is a mighty fine car you have there,' Herbert said.

'Yeah, keep your paws off. I usually don't do business with your type, but I need some rotten fruit. You have any?' the man asked.

'I have some fruit that went bad. But wouldn't you rather have some of our fresh, delicious pears? I picked them this morning. I must say, a man of your importance and stature deserves only the best.'

'Stop trying to hustle me. I'll give you half price for your rotten fruit. Now you have any or not.'

'Sure, I have some. But I can't charge you for rotten fruit. Why do you want rotten fruit anyway?'

'I'm going to throw it at my neighbor's house. He's always having family barbecues, laughing, and playing out in the yard. Maybe this will get him to move away. He is almost as annoying as you are.'

Herbert, sensing the man was upset, got up and tried to hug him.

'Hey, get away from me, you big hairy ape. You try that again, and I'll turn you into nothing but a hairball. What kind of monster are you?'

'Obviously not a very good one,' Herbert answered.

Herbert found the man's words hurtful, but he still had empathy for him. Also, in times of stress like this, his reverse Tourette's took over.

'That's a really nice shirt you are wearing. It gives you a nice trim look.'

This compliment caught the man off-guard. He had always had a weight problem and often tried to wear clothes that made him look thinner.

'Do you really think so? Not too loose around the shoulders?' the man asked.

Herbert and the man spent the better part of an hour talking. Herbert gave the man tips on how he could get along better with his neighbor. The man tried to teach Herbert how to snarl and generally be scarier.

They parted as friends, and Herbert gave him three of his freshest pears at no charge. Not much of a monster, not much of a businessman either.

As the man drove away, Herbert shouted, 'Have a Nice Day.'

A DATE WITH DESTINY

by Steve Lance

'Good news Delta, we are headed back to Earth,' said Sigma as he walked into Delta's workshop. 'I'm doing an advance class on probe techniques for some guys at Area 51. Can I borrow one of yours, the one with the green light? It gives off a nice eerie glow. I think you named it Big Daddy.'

'Oh yeah, Big Daddy,' Delta replied as he pulled it out of its case. 'Some of my finest work. The humans really like this one. You can borrow it, but make sure this time you clean it before you return it.'

'You want to come and watch? A group of government

bureaucrats running around with highly advanced anal probes, sure to give you a laugh or two,' ask Sigma.

'No, I think I'll just hang around the ship,' answered Delta.

'You should contact that girl you met the last time we were here. You know, the one you spent so much time talking to at that coffee shop you never got around to abducting,' said Sigma.

'Oh, Sharon, I don't know. She wasn't really into me.'

'Not into you. When I came in, she was rubbing your pointy little head, saying how cute you were. I almost barfed. Plus, the next three worlds we are due to visit are all Slug Worlds. I mean, humans are self-centered, egotistical beings, but they can be fun to be around. Remember that time we went to that Halloween frat party and won best costume? We weren't even wearing costumes. Tell me you didn't have a good time,' Sigma said.

Delta enjoyed meeting earth people. On most planets, there was only primeval sludge, lizard people, giant slugs, or Big Foot (note to self, recapture Big Foot, return him to his home planet before anyone sees him). It would be nice to go on a date with Sharon.

Delta contacted Sharon using telepathy. 'Hi Sharon, It's Delta. Do you remember me?'

'What? Who said that? Where are you?' asked a startled Sharon.

'It's me, Delta. We had coffee a couple weeks back. I'm communicating by thought.'

'Oh, the alien who was going to abduct me but got too busy and had to leave. Stuck me with the bill too.'

'Yeah, sorry about that, I only had Qubits. They wouldn't take them. Anyway, I'm going to be on Earth tomorrow and wanted to see if you wanted to go out?'

'Sorry, I'm washing my hair.'

'I'm reading your mind. I know that's a lie. Come on, some Laser Tag, what do you say.'

'Stop reading my mind. Why can't you call me on the cell like everyone else.'

'I'm outside the solar system. The cell rates are astronomical. Besides, this is easier. I can tell you are thinking yes.'

'Ok, pick me up at seven, and don't be late.'

Delta asked Sigma what she meant by seven. Sigma explained what clocks were and showed Delta a live feed of Big Ben. When the big hand was on twelve and the little hand on seven, he should teleport to Sharon's house in Chugwater, Wyoming.

When Delta got to Sharon's porch, the house was dark. He had to ring the bell several times before Sharon got to the door. She looked mad.

'Where have you been, and why are you knocking at midnight,' Sharon said.

Confused, Delta said, 'No, it's seven. See Big Ben, big hand, little hand.'

'That's 7:00 am, and it's in London. The time there differs from Wyoming. You should have been here five hours ago.'

'Sharon, time travels at the same rate all over the earth. Now, if we were on different planets, there could be a time difference, but on earth where the gravity is …'.

'Stop aliensplaining. You were supposed to be here five hours ago,' Sharon said and slammed the door.

Still feeling Sharon was wrong about how space-time worked, Delta knew he should not continue arguing. In the 'Human Dating Guide', he had read that the female species would make your life a living hell if you got them mad and continued to argue. He wondered why the females with such a great power did not simply conquer all the males and make them do their bidding.

Delta quickly returned to the ship, set the time distortion field back five hours, and returned to Sharon's porch. This time when he rang, Sharon answered right away.

'Hi Delta, you are looking nice, and seven o'clock, right on time,' said Sharon.

Delta handed Sharon a bouquet of snakes and a box of worms. He had read in the guide you should present a present to the female on your first date.

Sensing Sharon was nervous about the snakes, Delta said, 'Don't worry, only the ones that rattle are poisonous, and I included a small bottle of anti-venom in the ribbon. The worms are a delicacy on Planet Albatross. You should try one.'

'Ah, they look delicious, but I want to save them for a special occasion,' said Sharon.

Things were not off to a good start. Delta remembered the guide also said you should complement your date on some minor feature. 'You have very adequate feet, only a small amount of toe fungus, and the odor is well within acceptable parameters,' Delta said, smiling.

'Should we just go play some laser tag?' Sharon replied.

Delta and Sharon had a great time playing laser tag, although Delta was disappointed with the lasers power. He asked Sharon if he could grab a couple of lasers from the ship. They could vaporize the opponents with one shot. Sharon told him it wouldn't be sporting, and besides, they were doing just fine. Sharon was an excellent shot, and they easily won all their matches.

When they returned to Sharon's front porch, Delta said, 'In a few hours, someone who looks exactly like me is going to show up. Just ignore him. It's a space-time mix-up. It's not some late-night booty call.'

'Ok, sweety,' Sharon said and kissed him on the cheek.

Delta was disappointed that they only kissed on the cheek. He had captured a fly and had it rolled up in his tongue. If they had kissed on the lips, he was going to slip the fly to her as a prese

'Goodnight, and just remember to feed those snakes some mice, and they will do fine,' said Delta.

Back on the ship, Sigma asked, 'How was your date.'

'It was ok, but she only kissed me on the cheek when we left,' Delta replied.

'Ouch. By the way, don't do that thing with the tong' One of the government guys told me earth wom Strange creatures.'

'How did your class on advance probing techniques go?' asked Delta.

'Excellent, I have got some hilarious YouTube video,' said Sigma as the spaceship sped away.

THE SWAMP MONSTERS AND THE CASE OF THE MISSING ROBE

by Steve Lance

This year's Swamp Monster convention was being held in Washington DC. Spirits were high after the first day, primarily due to a pledge by the Keynote Speaker, Senator Bull Schmitt, that they had no intentions of actually draining the swamp. He went on to say he was 100% behind the swamp monsters and felt the real problem was all the sea monsters who kept coming ashore. That the sea monsters were illegally causing mayhem,

mayhem that should be the work of the swamp monsters. The Senator received a standing ovation.

But on the second day, during the mandatory session on "New Rules and Regulations on the Use and Clean Up of Slime", the hotel manager announced that one of the robes used at the swimming pool was missing. This was very troublesome since the swamp monsters were on a tight budget, and there were no extra funds to pay for a robe.

The budget problems mainly stemmed from the aforementioned sea monster cutting their rates on basic monster services such as dismemberment, beheadings, wedgies, and your standard, "Scaring the Shit out of People". They also had a two-for-one special on Tuesdays, which the swamp monsters could not match.

The perpetrator had to be found and found quickly. The attention first turned to Moe. Moe was the last one at the pool and had easy access to all the robes. But it was pointed out that Moe does not use robes, which is a significant problem because, after his showers, he runs "all natural" through the halls shouting, 'Don't mind me, just air drying'. This had led to several sexual harassment lawsuits and some pretty unflattering pictures on Instagram.

The attention quickly moved to Samantha. Samantha was a known kleptomaniac. As a youth, she had stolen half of the flatware from the local Denney's restaurant. Before smoking was outlawed, she had swiped ashtrays from every bar within a hundred-mile radius. However, during questioning, it became clear that it was not Samantha. She pointed out that the robe was terry cloth, and she would not be caught dead in anything other than a silk robe. This was confirmed by her ex-husband, who said, and I quote, "Yeah, that prima donna little #@$&$, who thinks her farts don't stink, only the best for her, too good for the rest of us. Tell her I want my Led Zeppelin album back."

This was going to be a tough case to crack. The swamp monsters took a break and headed to the bar. After a couple of beers, they decided to do a round of shots and ordered some tequila. It was then that the case was cracked wide open, and the culprit was revealed.

Mort, a relatively new member of the swamp monster guild, asked the bartender for a saltshaker and a slice of lemon. Seeing this, the rest of the swamp monsters immediately knew it was Mort; in fact, Mort was not a swamp monster. The lead swamp monster, Art, pulled the mask off Mort. Everyone gasped. Mort was a sea monster; he had been sent to infiltrate the swamp monsters. You see, a swamp monster would never use salt. It dries out their slime glands, but sea monsters love salt.

Art demanded to know who sent Mort. That's when the swamp monster's faith in government was shaken to the core. You see, it was Senator Bull Schmitt who sent Mort. He actually did plan to drain the swamp and build luxury high-rise condominiums in its place.

Simon, a rather simple-minded swamp monster, asked, 'But how can he lie to us? He has been in office for twenty years. Certainly, a politician of that status would never lie.'

The rest of the swamp monsters had a good laugh at Simon's expense.

CLOWN ISLAND

by Steve Lance

I knew there was a risk, but I was too cheap to pay for a professional clown. So, I put on the makeup and wig and entertained the guest at my ten-year-old daughter's birthday party. And if I say so myself, I think I did a pretty good job. I had balloon animals and told lots of jokes that got both laughs and groans. "Where do sheep get their haircut? At the bah-bah shop.", "Why did the chicken cross the road? Social distancing." Everyone had a good time.

Then the moment of truth, I went to take off my makeup, and it would not come off. I tried for over an hour, but no luck. I had been turned into an actual clown.

My wife entered the bathroom, saw what had happened, and

started throwing things.

'I knew this was going to happen. I told you to just hire a clown. But no, you wanted to save a dollar.'

'Well, your dad always said you were married to a clown,' I said, trying to lighten the mood.

She just glared at me and stormed out. My daughter came in with tears in her eyes.

'Daddy, are you going to be a clown from now on?'

'Sweetheart, no, I just need to scrub harder.'

'My teacher says once a person turns, they can not turn back. I'm supposed to report you to the police. Oh, daddy, they are going to take you away and put you on Clown Island.'

'No, no, no. We must tell no one. I can fix this.'

I guess I should fill you in on what has been happening. Five years ago, people who played the part of clowns started turning into actual clowns. It didn't happen 100% of the time, but it happened a lot. And it was not just birthday party clowns, but rodeo clowns, clowns at circuses, and actors on TV who played clowns. Even if you sang the song "Send in the Clowns" with too much feeling, you would risk turning into a clown. The better you were at playing a clown, the higher the risk. That's why I figured I could get away with it. I'm not a professional. I guess I just did too good of a job. Most likely, it was the bah-bah joke that gets them every time.

So, the Mayor decides he can't have a city with a bunch of clowns running around. He passes a law that all clowns are sent to Clown Island. Clown Island used to be called Devil's Island. You may remember, fifty years ago, there was an outbreak of people turning into little devils. Same thing, they sent them off to the Island. Except with all those little devils in one place, it turned into a real Sodom and Gomorrah. They had to napalm the whole place.

The clowns are much better behaved. I mean, you have your occasional pie in the face or someone getting sprayed with seltzer water, but mostly they sit around and sing "Everybody Loves a Clown".

Everybody loves a clown, so why can't you?

A clown has feelings, too

If you had a clown gig, you could get a work pass to come into the city. But once the gig was over, it was back to the island.

Three days passed before the knock on the door. My wife answered the door, and there were two police officers.

'We understand you have a clown living at this residence,' the first officer said.

'Why no, you must have the wrong place,' my wife said.

'Who is the guy sitting in the Lazy Boy? The one with the red nose, curly orange hair, and clown face.'

'Oh, that's my husband. But he's no clown, he has a cold, and the red hair is because he is Irish, and the face, it's always been that way. I know hideous, so why did I marry him, right? Will, when I met him in college, he could make a gourmet meal out of cheese wiz. That's when I fell in love. Thanks for checking, so long.'

She tried to close the door, but the Officer stopped her.

'We are going to have to look,' the second officer said.

Clowns were considered so annoying that if there was even a chance you had one in your house, the police could do a search.

'I found a coconut cream pie,' the first officer called out.

'That is for our desert,' my wife answered.

'Are you sure he is not planning to hit someone in the face with it? I will have to take this as evidence.'

'Coconut cream, not really my favorite. See if they have cherry,' the second officer said.

'Nope, just the coconut cream,' the first officer said.

'Just leave it,' the second officer said.

Just then, the second officer picked up a book from the table.

'We got him, "How to Make Balloon Animals." This here is professional clown paraphernalia. You, sir, have just won a one-way trip to Clown Island.'

Clown Island was an awful place. You were constantly getting hit with pies or seltzer water. There was only one car; to get anywhere, 20 clowns would crowd into it. Then there was the never-ending squeaking of balloons as they rubbed together when making animals. The worst part was Bozo ran the whole place.

I was quickly going mad. I had a happy clown face painted on me, but my lips formed a frown.

I was thinking about organizing the clowns and attacking the city. But if we won, it would be a city full of clowns, hardly an improvement. Nope, this called for clown genocide. I just needed a plan.

I decided I would replace the helium tanks with hydrogen. Then have a contest to see who could create the largest balloon animal. One match and we have roasted clown, with a side of evil laughter.

It was a sinister plan, but something had to be done. One clown followed me around, beeping a little handheld horn. Someone had to die.

The preparations were going great. Ronald McDonald had agreed to officiate. Everything was in place, but then the Joker found out. I was worried at first, but it turned out he liked the idea and agreed to help.

So, there you have it. On Halloween night, with the largest balloon animal contest ever held, I put on "Stuck in the Middle with You" and dropped a match on the judging table.

It started a chain reaction of explosions. The blast could be seen from space. Three towns over, they were picking rubber noses out of the trees.

Only me and the Joker made it off that Island alive.

HERBERT AND THE MONSTER GUILD

by Steve Lance

Herbert had one wish in life, to become the world's scariest monster. He knew he would need to become part of the Monster Guild to reach his goal. He had applied many times in the past but had always been rejected.

I should tell you at this point that Herbert was not your typical monster. You see, he was always smiling and giving people compliments. His favorite saying was 'Have a Nice Day'. For a human, this is not a problem – well, maybe a little bit – but it was a massive problem for a monster.

When the letter arrived from the Monster Guild, Herbert was

very nervous. This would determine his future.

We regret to inform you that your application to the Monster Guild has been rejected. It was determined that you are just too damn nice. Your Monster Likeability Index (MLI) was the highest ever recorded. We recommend you shave your fur and try to pass as a human.

Herbert was devastated. It was one of the few times he did not smile. He sat around his apartment watching TV, eating ice cream, and playing Desperado on a continuous loop.

After a few days, Herbert decided to go for a walk, it was pleasantly warm, and the sun was shining. A smile returned to his face. He saw an elderly couple. Herbert waved and shouted, 'Have a Nice Day'.

'Such a nice monster,' the couple said.

Herbert was back.

Since he was not part of the Monster Guild, he needed to find a way to make a living. He decided to sell life insurance. He knew about a large group of underinsured swamp monsters. He grabbed his briefcase and headed for the swamp.

'Alright, let me get this straight. I buy this insurance, then I eat the person, and you guys pay. Seems too good to be true,' said Abe, the swamp monster.

'No, the insurance is on you. In case you die,' Herbert tried to explain.

'What, someone is going to eat me! Who? You? I would like to see that, you big blue ball of fur. Bring it on.'

'No, Abe, I don't want to eat you. It's in case you have an accident or something.'

'Is that a threat? Are you threatening me? Oh, me and you, it's show time.'

Things were not going well for Herbert. Swamp monsters just did not understand proper estate planning.

'Look, Herbert, I like you. I want to help you out. I mean, you are a bit annoying with all that "Have a Nice Day" and smiling like an idiot all the time. But you are who you are, and I like that you embrace your inner kindness. That can be tough for a monster. Tell you what, there are a bunch of fishermen down by the dock, let's go down there, and I'll help you sell some of this insurance,' said Abe.

'Hello, sir. I hope you are having a nice day. I'm Herbert with the Tri-State Life Insurance Company. Have you ever considered what would happen to your family if you should have an untimely death? I can help you with that; for a low monthly fee, you can get a $100,000 policy with no medical check-up. Can I sign you up today?' Herbert asked the first fisherman he saw.

The man looked terrified, shook his head yes, and signed the papers immediately.

Herbert thought to himself, boy, that was easy. Not only did I sell my first policy, but I think I'm finally becoming scarier. Herbert didn't realize that Abe was behind Herbert, and while Herbert was all smiles, Abe did not have that problem. He was licking his chops and sharpening his claws. When Herbert asked the man to sign, Abe made the gesture that he would cut his throat if he didn't sign.

They spent all afternoon approaching fishermen, and everyone purchased a policy.

'Thank you, Abe, for coming with me. I guess I didn't need your help after all. Sorry, you had to stand in the background,' Herbert said.

'No problem there, my blue hair friend,' Abe said.

'Have a Nice Day,' Herbert said as Abe headed home.

Herbert was named Salesman of the Month. He had the biggest smile when they took a picture of him for the company newsletter.

He also won first place in a sales contest. The prize was a Cadillac.

Herbert may not be the scariest monster. But when he is wearing his sunglasses in his Cadillac, he might be the coolest.

CHECK PLEASE

by Steve Lance

When I first heard there was a virus going around that made people crave chocolate cake, I did not believe it. Of course, people like chocolate cake. Who does not want a nice big slice, but they would go into a frenzy and do anything to get the cake, no way.

So, I googled it. Sure enough, there it was, right on the internet. Apparently, once infected, you would stop at nothing to get a slice of chocolate cake. There were accounts of people crashing birthday parties and grabbing cake out of the hands of children. Other stories of people breaking into bakeries and gorging themselves. One man stole a truck full of Ding Dongs. He was last seen headed for the mountains, traveling at a high rate of speed. The details were chilling.

Bakers were arming themselves. Some put up large signs saying they did not have any chocolate cake. One baker shot a UPS man because he was licking his fingers. He figured since he was licking his fingers, he must have just eaten some chocolate cake and was looking for more. He would state later, "No UPS man would lick his fingers if he was just delivering packages. That is just gross."

There was another story that three Zombies had kidnapped a baker and were making him bake chocolate cakes 24 hours, 7 days a week. The account remains unconfirmed.

Still, I had doubts, so I searched YouTube and found a video of a man stuffing cake into his mouth as fast as he could. It had thousands of comments and likes. The evidence was becoming overwhelming.

I turned on the TV and watched a congressional hearing with our nation's top health nutritionist. He stated that there was no medical evidence that a virus could cause someone to lose control and aggressively eat chocolate cake.

The congressmen were ready with a blistering cross-examination.

"Sir, have you yourself ever eaten chocolate cake?" asked the congressman.

"Yes," he said.

"On more than one occasion." The congressman continued.

"Well, yes, but that doesn't mean....," he said.

"A yes or no will do," Interrupted the Congressman.

"You may not be aware of this, but a vast majority of Americans like chocolate cake. Some of them say it is their favorite dessert. Unfortunately, there is also an obesity crisis in our great country, undoubtedly from eating too much chocolate cake. Now I have no doubt that this whole crisis has been caused by the current administration's incompetents. I plan to introduce legislation outlawing the consumption of chocolate cake." The congressman stated.

"Now, hold on." A second congressman piped in. "Americans have a right to eat any type of cake they want. This is clearly an overreach by our colleagues from the other side of the aisle, aimed at scaring hard-working Americans and taking away their God-given rights."

A third congressman stated he did not even like cake. "Apple pie was the real American dessert. Anyone who had cake instead of pie got what they deserved." He said that he heard members of the opposition party had gone as far as to serve those little finger cakes at the last 4th of July celebration.

They were all making good points. I was not sure what to think.

Just then, a news bulletin came over the air. California had just ordered that all Little Debbie's snack cakes be destroyed. They claimed it was out of an "abundance of caution". People had till 5 pm to turn in their snack cakes to the local police department. Afterward, they would fine anyone caught with a snack cake.

That evening as my wife and I were having dinner at our favorite restaurant, I told her it felt like the country I grew up in was slipping away. That I missed my childhood when it did not matter if you like cake or pie. We respected each other's choices.

Just then, the waitress came. She asked if we would like dessert.

"No, just the check," I said sadly.

SHARK TALES

by Steve Lance

"Hey Bret, what do you call a swimmer with no legs," shouted Sam the Shark.

"Ugh, don't start up again. You are not funny," replied Bret.

"A Weeble, get it," said Sam. "Come on, they wobble but don't fall down. You know that's funny."

"Hey, why is it that all the plump swimmers stay on the beach, and all we get are the skinny chicken leg ones."

"Leave the swimmers alone. I don't want to end up on the TV News again," said Bret.

Sam shrugged Bret off and switched the subject. "Hey, did you hear what happened to Jimmy? He was swimming by one of those shark cages, the ones those pervert marine biologists use when they want to spy on us. Well, they tagged him with one of those tracking devices. Got him right in the tush."

"Yeah, I saw him a few minutes ago. He was trying to get me to remove it," said Bret, "I told him sorry dude, we are friends and all, but that's a little too personal. If it wasn't in the tush, I would help a shark out, but I have to pass on this one. Next thing you know, he will want me to check his prostate."

"That's a good one," said Sam. "Look who the comedian is now."

Sam suddenly got an idea and swam up beside Bret. "Hey, you know what we should do. We should get all the sharks who have been tagged. There must be a few hundred; put them in an attack formation, something like a flying wedge, and have them head for a busy beach. It would freak the people out. I mean, think how they overreact when they see one dorsal fin swim past a beach. This would be epic."

Bret got a big smile on his face, well, as much as a shark can smile, so more like a toothy crazy grin. "Yeah, just think, it would take over a week for them to gather. All that time, the biologist screens would show those blinking blips slowly converging on some beach. They wouldn't know what to make of it. There would be emergency meetings, and they would have to inform the President. And all because they shot Jimmy in the tush."

"It would teach them a lesson. Let them know we have had enough, and you better not mess with us anymore," Sam said. "Hey, Jimmy, get over here."

Jimmy came swimming over, "Hey Sam, can you help me out? I

got tagged. It's really uncomfortable. Please pull it out."

"Sorry big guy, no can do. But I have a mission for you. We are going to teach those shark tagging, tush pokers a lesson. We need you to get together all the sharks who have been tagged and meet us near the Jersey Shore. When we get done with them, no one else will have to suffer the humiliation you are enduring," Sam said as he tried to rally Jimmy to the cause.

"I don't know, guys. I just want this thing removed. Can't one of you just pull it out?" Jimmy pleaded.

"We could," said Bret. "But then who would lead this critical mission? Now how long do you think it will take for you to contact everyone who has been tagged and get them to the Jersey Shore."

Looking bewildered, Jimmy said, "Months or years, I don't even think it's possible. I don't want to lead no mission. I'm not a leader. I just want my life back. Come on, one of you, pull it out."

"Months or years, that's going to be a problem. We don't have that kind of time," said Bret.

"Yeah, I didn't think of that. But wait, I got another idea," said Sam. "Jimmy, If I pull it out, can I have the tracking device."

"Sure, it's all yours. Just get it off of me," Jimmy replied.

"Now, Jimmy, If I pull it out, you also have to do something for me," Sam said while looking very seriously at Jimmy. "You have to take it, go up to the Jersey Shore, and tag Bruce Springsteen with it."

"What," cried Bret.

"Hear me out," continued Sam. "We tag Bruce, which means we can trace his whereabouts. Then, we sell that information to the paparazzi. They will pay big bucks."

"Why do we need money," said Bret looking confused.

"Ah, part two of my plan," said Sam. "We use the money to hire a sushi chef. No more eating mundane fish. From now on, only the finest prepared tuna, by the best chef money, can buy."

Jimmy was quick to agree. "Sure, sure, whatever you want. Just get it off me."

"Ok, come here, turn around, and assume the position," Sam instructed.

"Wow, there is a lot of cellulite back here. You may want to cut back on the sardines, maybe a little more cod instead."

After a little bit of difficulty, Sam freed Jimmy from the tracking device. He turned and handed Jimmy the device. "Now it's your turn. Fulfill our bargain."

Jimmy took the device and said, "Sorry guys, but I have to go, but thanks for getting this off of me." With that, he darted away.

Sam, looking discussed, shouted, "welcher."

Bret broke out laughing. "Never trust a shark. It wouldn't have worked anyway."

BOOKS BY THIS AUTHOR

A Shot In The Dark

A collection of short stories from emerging author Steve Lance.

These stories run the full gamut, from a commentary on societal problems to light-hearted humor.

In his debut book, you meet a wide variety of characters. Many of them sharing the midwestern values of the writer.

You will spend time with an old man trying to save his farm, a young girl called upon to protect her town, a couple deeply in love, and many more engaging characters.

Made in the USA
Middletown, DE
30 August 2022

71821586R00046